Two Days in November

A TEATIME TALES
NOVELETTE

LEENIE BROWN

Leenie B Books
Halifax

ISBNs: 978-1-989410-79-0 (ebook); 978-1-990607-39-4 (paperback); 978-1-990607-40-0 (large print)

www.leeniebbooks.com

www.leeniebrown.com

Chapter 1

18 November 1811

Monday dawned with all the brightness of a cloudless day and an abundance of female felicitations. Fitzwilliam Darcy welcomed the brightness of the day. The greetings from his host's sisters, he did not.

"Good morning, Mr. Darcy." Caroline Bingley hurried to reach the step he was on as he descended Netherfield's grand staircase. "It is a glorious morning for a walk in the garden. Is it not, Louisa?"

"Indeed, it is," Louisa Hurst agreed with her younger sister. "You should join us, Mr. Darcy."

"I am afraid I cannot. As you can see, I am dressed for riding."

"Are you?" Louisa cried. "I had not noticed. I suppose it was the beauty of the sun shining through the window above the door, as well as the knowledge that I will be able to enjoy a morning ramble without being interrupted by guests, that had my mind occupied so much that I did not notice your attire."

That was highly unlikely. Louisa could, at any given moment, recite the sweet delights of a particular garment worn by a stranger she had only seen for a few moments in passing, and in the next instant, she could overflow with caustic vitriol about the hatpin so and so had dared to pair with a hat of one style or another. She had seen what he was wearing.

"It is dreadfully quiet with just us at Netherfield now, do you not think?" Caroline asked.

"I did not find the Miss Bennets to be a particularly boisterous pair of guests." Both Miss Bennet and Miss Elizabeth had been charming and made no demands that they be entertained.

"You did not sit with dear, sweet Jane," Caroline replied.

Dear, sweet Jane had been dear and sweet to Caroline and Louisa when she arrived and when she left. However, between those times, she had been a source of discontent, but not because Miss Bennet was disagreeable or demanding. It was that she had a sister who was both enchanting and caring enough to tend to dear sweet Jane while she convalesced.

"Did Miss Bennet talk incessantly?" he asked, though he knew full well that she was not the sort to do so.

Louisa giggled. "No, that particular quality is the domain of her mother and youngest sisters."

Darcy cringed as Louisa's thoughts mirrored his own, and he had no desire to be easily compared to Mrs. Hurst.

Caroline tittered. "Indeed! Miss Lydia is the worst of the lot with her ceaseless talking about balls and officers! The youngest Miss Bennets would never be accepted anywhere in town. They are far too unrefined."

Again, Darcy flinched as another of Bingley's sisters voiced his thoughts. How had he come to this? He had not been raised to be so disparaging of others.

"Miss Lydia is a good number of years younger than Miss Bennet," he said. "Perhaps with time, she will improve."

He placed his hat on his head and prepared to take his leave. He had had his fill of taunts and teases about the Bennets last evening. He had had his fill of casting his own barbs. Indeed, as he listened to Caroline and Louisa this morning, he was rightly ashamed of himself. He did not wish to begin his day with more of the same.

In fact, he would like nothing better than to think on things other than Bennet ladies – well, one Bennet lady in particular, the one who was enchanting and caring, the one who was provoking Louisa and Caroline to oppose the entire Bennet family, the one who, had she better connections, would warrant their jealousy. However, as it was, Miss Elizabeth Bennet was a pretty lady to admire but not to pursue. No matter how much Darcy found himself wishing to do just that. And that was why he desperately needed to find something else about which to think.

Louisa gasped. "You defend her? Caroline, it is worse than we imagined. Shall we write the announcement for the paper?"

"What announcement?" he asked, though he was not so stupid as to not understand Louisa's meaning. "I know of nothing to announce."

"Why! It is only a matter of time until you have been trapped by Mrs. Bennet and tied to one of her daughters," Louisa answered.

"With any luck, it will be the fine-eyed Elizabeth." There was an acerbic edge to Caroline's jibe.

"I will thank you not to plan my future for me. I shall not be trapped by anyone." He looked pointedly at Caroline for she was the most determined, teasing flirt when he was around her. "Good morning to you both."

And with that, he took his leave of them and Netherfield's house.

Twenty minutes of riding in solitude later, he finally felt the presence of Bingley's sisters slide from his shoulders and tumble down the field behind him as his horse raced along it. Feeling lighter, he slowed his horse to a walk and inhaled the tranquility of his surroundings. For several minutes he rode, taking in the vistas and views without a single, solitary care pricking his mind and interrupting the indulgence. However, those cares could not be held off for long. His was a mind that was continually working on something. It rarely stood idle or allowed itself to be filled with emptiness.

Of course, when his mind could be no longer be held at bay, it returned to his most recent topic of contemplation, Miss Elizabeth. It was her laughing eyes and smiling lips that first invaded the blissful serenity of his ride. They called to him, begging him to defy whatever she had just said, while her light and pleasing figure taunted him to dance with her, to hold her hand, and to draw her along a garden path to a secluded arbor where he and she could be alone. Whether awake or asleep, these visions tormented him. It was a disturbing reality into which he had fallen, and the most troubling part of his current existence was that Caroline had been right about something earlier. He did find Netherfield dull. Ever since yesterday, after returning from services, Netherfield had felt devoid of life.

He had struggled to occupy himself with anything for any length of time yesterday. Bingley had even beaten him handily in a game of billiards.

Darcy would wonder what had become of him if it were not for the fact that he already suspected he knew. He was almost certain he had fallen in love with Miss Elizabeth Bennet. He had not intended to allow such a thing to happen. He had even taken care on Saturday to not speak to her or even look at her more than he absolutely had to. Yet, he had not avoided the danger of his heart being entangled.

All was not lost, however. Miss Elizabeth was gone. She was at her home, and three miles separated them. He would see her on occasion, but he would not be constantly in her presence. This weak longing, this infantile infatuation, this ember of love, would grow weaker and be extinguished soon.

But, his heart argued, why must it be so?

"Father married for love," he said to the morning breeze. "Your mother's pedigree was exceptional. She had a fortune and ties to the powerful Earl of Matlock." He quoted what his father had often said to him when discussing his future as master of Pemberley and his need to choose a wife. At the time, choosing a wife was years in the future, as, he had also thought, was the day when he would take his father's place. Unfortunately, he had only been right about one of those things. His need for a wife had not been hastened, but his role as Master of Pemberley had been thrust upon him much sooner than he had been prepared to take it.

He smiled as he remembered his mother and the way his father's face would soften when speaking of her. Theirs was a match which others envied. There were no whispers of lovers or discontent. There could not have been any, for theirs was an ardent love – fine and stout, unbendable, and with a constancy that outlived life itself.

Be that as it may, there was one grievance that entered their marriage and remained even after his mother had died. Lady Catherine. Darcy's aunt. His mother's only sister.

"A gentleman does not just marry a lady. He joins himself to a family forever." That, along with a "take care where you allow your heart to go," was how his father had always ended their discussion.

And that was why his heart was not to be encouraged in its desires for Miss Elizabeth. Her fortune was small – if it could even be called a fortune in the most generous use of the word. Her pedigree was littered with individuals, who, though they might be decent enough people, held a lower status in society than he did. Those two complaints were not overly grievous. He needed no propping up of his accounts, nor was he so high in the step as to shun any connection to trade. It was that final admonition from his father about joining himself to a family that was the hinge on which his disapproval of Miss Elizabeth as his wife swung.

He could not entirely fault Caroline or Louisa for their disparagements of the Bennets, for the criticism was not fabricated out of bits of fluff and fancy. Mrs. Bennet was boisterous. Her youngest daughters were left unchecked. And Mr. Bennet seemed incapable of managing either his estate or his family. Perhaps another man could overlook such things, but to Darcy, they were enough to make him challenge his heart. Love could not be enough in this case, could it be?

Just as his heart was arguing with him that love had supported his father when faced with the annoyance that was Aunt Catherine, Darcy crested a hill and saw the lady whom he was attempting to forget. She was sitting on a stile, her bonnet rested on the stone wall next to her, and she seemed to be watching something most intently.

He should turn around and return to Netherfield. He should not go in her direction. It was folly to even think he could safely stop and talk to her. Yet, despite all that he knew he should not do, he walked his horse in her direction.

As he approached, she glanced over her shoulder. Where was her quick smile? Her face turned away from him, and he saw her brush at her cheeks. Was she crying?

"Are you well, Miss Elizabeth?" His heart was pounding, and he seemed unable to dismount his horse quickly enough.

She stood and curtseyed. "I am well, Mr. Darcy. I am just a bit melancholy this morning."

She was not well. Her cheeks were damp, and her eyes and nose were red. She had not shed only a few tears. Whatever was troubling her was more than a touch of melancholy.

"Please, be seated. I do not wish to take you from your repose." He now stood across the stile from her. "May I join you for a few moments?"

Her eyes grew wide, and she blinked twice before she answered. It was as if the thought of him wishing to spend time with her was shocking.

"Of course," she stammered, stepping to the side so he could cross the stile. "However, I fear I will not be pleasant company."

Having crossed the stile, he chose a grassy spot and sat down while Miss Elizabeth retook her seat. He tried to ignore her look of bewilderment by leaning back on his hands and gazing toward the sky.

"I do not ask to join you so that you can entertain me as one would a guest in her sitting room." He glanced at her. "You appear to be carrying a heavy burden, and I only wish to offer my assistance."

Oh, he knew he was tossing himself directly in danger's path, but she looked so vulnerable that he simply had to make some attempt to comfort her. He would not be able to live with himself if he were to see her so distraught and ride away. Therefore, he would brave the possibility of a stronger attachment, one which may not ever be able to be broken, being formed.

"Will you share it with me? Your burden?"

He sat quietly as she smoothed her skirts and fidgeted with the sleeve of her pelisse. Finally, she drew a breath and nodded.

Chapter 2

Darcy waited patiently to hear what Elizabeth had to say. Whatever it was, it appeared to be taking some thought before sharing.

"You have been in company with my sister Jane," Miss Elizabeth began. "Surely, you must have some idea of how gentle and kind she is."

"I do." From what Darcy had seen of her, Miss Bennet was pleasantness personified, which did make him wonder how she could be the cause of her sister's distress. Unless, of course, what she appeared to be was not what she was.

"And I am certain her beauty has not gone unnoticed."

"She is beautiful." No one could meet Jane Bennet without noting her classic beauty.

"Do you not wonder why a lady so beautiful and pleasant remains unwed at the advanced age of twenty-three?"

He shook his head. "I have not even thought to consider it."

In truth, he had not considered age or beauty when thinking about Miss Bennet's marital state as it applied to his friend, who seemed besotted with her. Darcy had only considered her family, her fortune, and her reception and return of Bingley's attentions.

"I have heard," from Caroline and Louisa, more than once, "that she has not had a season." It was a grievous mark against dear, sweet Jane according to Bingley's sisters. "Therefore, I assumed it was the lack of a suitable gentleman." One with enough money to please Mrs. Bennet is what he had thought.

"She may not have had a London season, but she has not lacked for suitors. There are acceptable, and some would even say preferable, gentlemen in the country."

Her tone was sharp, so he leaned forward and regarded her intently, trying his best to convey his sincerity in his expression. "Forgive me. I did not mean to offend. I am a man of the country, as well as a man of town. In truth, I find the country preferable to town in many ways, though not all. London does afford many things that Derbyshire does not."

Her brow furrowed as she studied him for a moment. "I apologize, Mr. Darcy, but I do not yet fully understand your character. It is so different at times from what I first thought it was."

Well, yes, he had likely not made the best first impression on her.

She continued her scrutiny of him for a moment before she continued. "I do not mean to offend, sir, but I must be certain that I am assessing your character correctly."

"I understand."

"If I choose to place my trust in you, will you treat it and what I tell you with respect?"

Shock suffused his features before he could stop it. He knew her first impression of him had been poor, but to be thought of as one who told tales and toyed with the trust another would put in him? That rankled. "I assure you,

Miss Elizabeth, that I am a respectable gentleman who is not given to gossip." He worked diligently to keep any offense he felt from his voice.

"I apologize for asking such a pointed question of you, Mr. Darcy, but there are those who would find the suffering of the unpolished members of country society to be fertile grounds for disparagement. I cannot, whether knowingly or by chance, subject my sister to such treatment. Therefore, I needed to be certain of your honour."

If her words were meant to reprimand him for the behaviour of Bingley's sisters, as well as his own, they had found their mark. Had he not participated in jesting about the people of Hertfordshire with Caroline and Louisa? Had he not, while in a fit of pique, acted the part of one who was above others at the assembly? He had. He knew he had, and it pricked his conscience.

However, the discomfort he experienced upon hearing Miss Elizabeth's words was not fully explained by his poor behaviour. The smart he felt was also because he knew the need to protect a sister from those who would do her harm – be it in word or deed – and yet he had not applied that knowledge to the sisters of others. He truly had been arrogant and thoughtless!

That behaviour must cease. Beginning with Miss Elizabeth and her sisters. Even the youngest ones.

"I understand, Miss Elizabeth. I would not place my sister in such a position." Not for any inducement. "And I will not do it with yours."

She held his gaze. Then, apparently finding whatever she had been searching for in his expression, she turned her head to the left.

"Do you see where Jane sits?"

Miss Bennet was here? Darcy followed Miss Elizabeth's line of sight. Sure enough. There was Miss Bennet, sitting on a fallen tree not far from the road. How had he missed seeing her?

"That tree is the reason she is not yet wed."

Darcy's eyebrows knit together. "A tree prevented your sister from acquiring a suitable match?" He had heard many things blamed for why one lady or another was not wed, but a tree? That was a new one.

Miss Elizabeth shook her head. "No, that tree did not prevent her from acquiring a suitable match. She had one. It took him from her. Two years ago, today."

She sighed while Darcy expelled a small burst of air much like he did when his sparring partner at Gentleman Jackson's landed a soft punch to his abdomen when he was not expecting it.

"I am sure you met the Gouldings at the assembly since Mrs. Goulding has a daughter who is to come out this year and you have a fortune." Miss Elizabeth raised an eyebrow while her lips lifted in a small wry smile. "Mrs. Goulding is as much on the hunt for a worthy husband for her daughter as my mother is for my sisters and me."

His eyes widened. If she wished him to reply in some fashion to such a comment, she was going to be disappointed because he had no idea how to reply graciously to what she had just said.

She chuckled. "Yes, Mr. Darcy, I know what my mother is, but I also know why she is as she is. My father's estate is entailed." She let that simple statement be the full explanation of why her mother would be so eager to have her daughters marry well.

Entails could be a messy business, depending on how marriage papers and portions set aside had been managed. He hoped that Mr. Bennet had made some sort of proper provision for his wife and daughters, but, if he had not, he would not be the first gentleman to have neglected such a thing. Why, just last year, Darcy had heard some lady decrying how she was doing her best to see two young ladies well-matched since their brother, a son from their father's first marriage, had seen fit to give his stepmother and sisters little to live on since he was not required to give them more.

Miss Elizabeth's smile faded as she stared once more at her sister. A shadow passed over her face, stealing the light from her eyes and leaving in its place a deep sadness.

Darcy wanted to place his hand on hers, to offer some little amount of comfort, but he could not. It was not his place to be so familiar. He could only listen as she quietly began to relate her story while fighting to retain control of her emotions.

"Two years ago, Robert Goulding, Mrs. Goulding's eldest son, stole my sister's heart. She was completely and utterly besotted. She quite openly demonstrated her admiration for him, and he was no less open about his affection for her. They were seen together in public often, and at every assembly, he would dance the opening and closing sets with her – and other than myself and Miss Lucas, who was the sister of his dearest friend, he refused to stand up with any other lady."

Darcy could not help but smile at the image of such a besotted fellow. Bingley seemed well on his way to be being just as enamoured with Miss Bennet as Mr. Goulding had been.

"As you might imagine," Miss Elizabeth continued, "it was not long until he petitioned my father for her hand and was granted permission to present his offer. Jane, of course, accepted him with alacrity. The date was set for after the banns were read, and that evening, a celebration dinner was enjoyed by all at Longbourn."

Miss Elizabeth absent-mindedly fingered the edge of her handkerchief. The difficulty of relating her tale was palpable. Again, Darcy had to resist the urge to offer her some sort of comfort. It was agony to only sit and listen.

"It had rained many days in the previous fortnight, and due to the deplorable condition of the roads and a threatening storm, my father invited Mr. Goulding to remain at Longbourn for the night. However, Mr. Goulding was overcome with enthusiasm for his prospects and wished to return home to share his joy with his family. So, he set off, promising to return on the morrow."

She blew out a breath, drew another, and released that one as well. "He never returned." The words were little more than a whisper.

This time, Darcy could not refrain from taking her hand. She looked at him curiously, and he squeezed her hand and waited for her to try to withdraw it from his, but she did not. She allowed him to continue to hold her hand as she resumed her story.

"He was found, lying beside the road where that tree lies now. The storm broke just as he was riding home, and it is speculated that the tree, upon which Jane sits, was brought down during the storm, frightening his horse." She closed her eyes and swallowed. Her fingers gripped his more firmly. "They say the horse threw him, and the impact as he landed fractured his neck. His death was mercifully quick." A tear slipped down her cheek and was quickly wiped away.

"Jane comes here to remember him. She does not visit as often as she once did, and today may prove to be her last visit; for today, she comes to release him."

"Forgive me, but I do not understand. If Mr. Goulding is no longer living, has he not already been released?" Darcy kept his voice soft because he did not wish to distress her further.

"He has been released from this earthly vale of sorrows, but he has not been released from Jane's heart." She looked at Darcy. "Though there have been many who have attempted to win her affections, she has been afraid to open herself to another. However, she has recently found a reason to consider allowing herself to seek again the happiness she once had."

He knew she was speaking of his friend. Yet her response puzzled him. "I would think that such a thing would make you happy, not melancholy. I would be pleased to see my sister regain her heart after a tragedy." His mind turned to his own sister and her recent despondence. He longed to see her emerge from her sad existence.

"Perhaps, if I did not fear she would be injured in doing so, I could be happy, but I do fear for her."

"What do you fear?"

She drew her hand away from his. "The answer may be considered offensive to some."

Bingley.

"What do you fear about my friend?"

"I fear his constancy, or more precisely, his lack of constancy." She pressed her lips together as if keeping the rest of what she wanted to say from escaping.

"Your fears are not without grounds." Bingley did tend to flit from lady to lady both because he was charming and amiable and because his heart had not yet been touched. He also struggled to determine if a lady liked him or his money. "My friend is charming and is easily amused. Those things can indicate a fickle heart in some. Added to that, Mr. Bingley does have a habit of seeking my opinion more often than he ought, and his sisters do hold more sway over him than is proper."

Her eyes were wide with surprise.

"Are these facts the basis for your fears?"

She nodded.

"Just as you know what your mother is, I know what my friend is."

Her posture relaxed, and a small smile tugged at her mouth for a moment, then was gone.

"I fear Jane will put her hope in a hopeless situation, and her heart will, once again, be shattered. I do not know how often a heart can endure such pain before it becomes unable to mend."

"A hopeless situation? Bingley is certainly capable of being constant." In fact, he was the most loyal friend a fellow could have.

"That may be. However, though I live in the country, I am not unaware of how society thinks about marriage. Jane's small portion and her ties to trade would not help increase Mr. Bingley's standing in the ton as a newly landed gentleman. In Hertfordshire, it would matter little, but in town, amongst your circles, I cannot see a match with my sister doing him any favours. In addition to that fact, it is no secret to me that, though they pretend to accept Jane, his sisters are not highly agreeable to the match. A union between our family and theirs would certainly not help Miss Bingley's chances of making an advantageous match outside of our small sphere. Even if your friend loves my sister as much as she loves him, I do not see how a happy future can be the result of their marrying."

Darcy simply stared at her for a moment. Her thoughts so closely mirrored his own. He worried about Bingley's happiness in marriage. Of course, he had worried more that Bingley would find himself in a marriage of unequal affections than that he would find himself in one of unequal fortunes. "Your sister is a gentleman's daughter – the fact that her relations are in trade does not alter that fact."

"While that may be true, you know that one gentleman's daughter is not looked at the same as another gentleman's daughter. Money and connections play a part."

Oh, he knew that. He had been telling himself something similar for days now as he tried to dissuade himself of the notion that Miss Elizabeth would be a good choice as his wife. His father's final cautions about marriage played in his mind.

"But if they loved each other – most ardently – would that not be enough to weather whatever trials family, fortune, and society might pose?" His heart thumped wildly as he waited for her answer, for he was not only asking on behalf of his friend but also to find an answer for himself.

"For Jane, it would be. She does not need the approval of her friends and family in the same way that your friend seems to. I fear he will be dissuaded from his suit before the attachment can grow strong enough."

It was a valid concern, and one Darcy would investigate. He would not knowingly allow his friend to cause pain for Miss Bennet. It did not matter what others thought about the union. What was of utmost importance was what Bingley thought.

Darcy's head tipped as understanding dawned on him about his own situation. It was not just his friend who sought the approval of others. He, himself, was doing the same when he dismissed his feelings for Elizabeth. He smiled as he realized that his head finally agreed with his heart. Marrying Elizabeth was not imprudent. He did not need her wealth or her status to further himself in society. He had attempted to find a societally approved match, but he had not met with success for he could not and would not tie himself to an arrangement that was less than what his father and mother's marriage had been.

He had found the lady he loved. She sat in front of him, watching him and waiting for him to respond to what she had said. To put her aside simply because he feared a few unpleasant visits with her family or the whispers of those ladies of the ton who would be disappointed to have lost their chance to snare Pemberley was foolishness fit only to be lauded in the halls of his Aunt Catherine's home of Rosings.

"It seems, then, that we shall just have to see that Bingley is not dissuaded."

"You would promote such a union?"

The shock in her voice told him a great deal about how she viewed him. Had he truly made such a dreadful impression? Steps must be taken to alter her opinion, for he was resolved to not only aid his friend in finding happiness in marriage, but he was also determined to secure the same for himself.

"I would promote such a match if it is one in which love truly exists. I have seen enough advantageous marriages that cause nothing but misery for all involved, and I would never wish such an existence on my friend."

The clouds that had darkened her eyes seemed to lift, and she smiled happily. "I still do not know what to make of your character, Mr. Darcy, but I believe I like it. Shall we embark on this project together? You can encourage your friend to make his own choices while I guard my sister's heart until I know the danger is gone?"

He extended his hand and shook hers. "Partners," he said. "Should we think of a name for this project and perhaps a code to communicate without being suspected by your sister or my friend?"

Elizabeth laughed. "You make it sound like a game that children would play."

"I will admit that it is not unlike those games in which my cousin and I engaged when we were children, but I ask you, must games be confined to the young? I only hope our project will be as enjoyable as those games of our youth."

"It shall be so long as we are successful." Elizabeth's cheeks grew rosy. "I am loath to admit it, but I was never a gracious loser."

Darcy chuckled. "Then we have something in common, Miss Elizabeth. Do you remember when I said my temper was too little yielding? I fear it has been so since I was young, though I hope I have brought it under good regulation as an adult."

There was a twinkle of mirth in Elizabeth's eyes and humour in her voice. "Did you sulk and pout when you lost a game, Mr. Darcy, or did you seek vengeance?"

"I did not pout."

"But you sulked and sought vengeance?" She was clearly struggling not to laugh.

How light his heart felt to see her smiling and laughing again, even if it was at his expense. "I like to think I sought justice rather than vengeance. And you? Did you sulk and pout or seek vengeance?"

She grimaced. "All three. As much as I would like to think I have brought such sentiments under good regulation, I am ashamed to say that my temper is still too quick and my ability to forgive too slow. It has always been a constant battle, though I no longer resort to pulling hair and hiding bonnets." She smiled wryly and shook her head. "It really is understandable why my mother complains about my trying her nerves. I am afraid I was not an easy child, very unlike Jane."

"Children may be similar, but they are rarely the same. My sister, Georgiana, is exceptionally gentle. She speaks softly and rarely in haste even when provoked, while I, on the other hand, am more apt to offend."

Her eyes held his. Approval was in their depths. "You care for her a great deal."

"I do." He stood and looked in Jane's direction. "And you care for her a great deal."

She rose from her spot on the stile, so he could step over it. He took his horse's reins and turned to her. "Miss Elizabeth, it has been a pleasure to speak with you. I shall return to Netherfield and see how the north wind blows while you tend to the southern seas."

Her eyebrows drew together in question. He looked to his left and right before leaning towards her and whispering, "The code."

She caught a giggle by pressing her fingers against her lips. "Of course, the code." She waited as he mounted his horse. "Thank you, Mr. Darcy. I do feel as if a burden has been lessened."

He touched his hat and nodded. "My pleasure." Then, after giving a cluck and a nudge to his horse, he rode off toward Netherfield.

Chapter 3

19 November 1811

"FINALLY," CHARLES BINGLEY MUTTERED as he and Darcy rode away from Netherfield. "I thought I would never be rid of my sisters."

"They have seemed to be everywhere as of late," Darcy agreed. All day yesterday, he had attempted to have a private conversation with Bingley regarding Miss Bennet, but every time he came close to shifting the topic of discussion to Miss Bennet, one or another of Bingley's sisters would interrupt them with some question.

"They are not in town, so there is very little to keep them occupied." He shot Darcy a look that said that even if there were a hundred things for Caroline and Louisa to do in Hertfordshire, they would not be happy.

"Yes, there is nothing more to do here than what they would do at Pemberley," Darcy answered dryly, causing Bingley to laugh.

"You would think that a lady, who is set on marrying a gentleman who does not just own a country house but also lives in said country house for a good part of the year, would attempt to appear more content with her surroundings than Caroline does."

"I have no intention of marrying your sister whether she can be content at Netherfield or not."

Bingley laughed. "I do not expect you to marry her. I would prefer to see you happily wed. Caroline would only drive you to distraction and cause strife. Even you cannot forebear her foolishness with good grace forever."

"Not even Job would have enough patience for Caroline," Darcy muttered. She had never annoyed him as much as she currently did.

"Ho, now! I think that is the first time I have heard you disparage her so directly. Has she done something to anger you?"

Darcy shook his head. "No, I was just imagining the distractions of yesterday, multiplied by every day until I die."

"She did herself no favour by being ever-present yesterday, did she?"

"Not at all." Her caustic tone whenever she spoke of Bingley's neighbours, especially the eldest Miss Bennets, did her even less good. "I had hoped to discuss something with you that I did not wish for her to hear."

"Have you found someone to marry?" Bingley asked with a grin.

"That was not exactly what I wished to discuss with you," Darcy said, neatly avoiding giving a direct answer to Bingley's question. He had found a lady he would like to marry, but he was not ready to admit that to Bingley. "However, I would like to let my horse run for a distance before we take up the topic on which I wish to hear your thoughts."

"I suppose my curiosity can wait to be satisfied so long as you agree to ride through Meryton."

"Through Meryton?" Darcy glanced at his friend. "Is there a reason?"

"Miss Bennet and her sisters might walk to town today."

"How do you know this?"

Bingley shrugged. "I do not know that they will. I just hope they will and that we can meet them by chance."

"Would it not be better to ride toward Longbourn?"

Bingley shook his head. "That last evening when Miss Bennet was at Netherfield, she mentioned that she needed some trim for the dress she intends to wear to my ball. She also said she thought she would be well enough to walk into town by today. Then, she told me when she left Netherfield that she only needed a partial day of rest and she would be all set to right."

Miss Bennet had been well enough to take a walk yesterday, not that Darcy was going to share that information with his friend. Elizabeth had trusted him with her secret fears for her sister, and he would do nothing to endanger that trust. And so, he allowed Bingley to choose where they would run and which approach they would make to Meryton.

"Have you rested long enough?" Bingley asked as the two of them rode into Meryton.

They had stopped racing several minutes ago, but neither had spoken as they gave themselves and their horses time to recover from the exertion.

"My curiosity can only be put off for so long," he added.

Darcy chuckled. Bingley was an inquisitive and impatient fellow at times.

As they turned onto High Street, Darcy was almost certain he saw Elizabeth and her sisters standing in front of a shop, conversing.

"Is that not Miss Bennet?" he asked.

Bingley darted a look around him, trying to find her. He most certainly seemed rightly besotted.

"In front of the milliner's shop," Darcy added.

"I say, Darcy! Good eye! It is indeed Miss Bennet. I think I would know her figure anywhere. She is a beauty, is she not?"

"That is what I wished to speak to you about. Is her beauty all that you find to recommend her?"

Bingley slowed his horse further and looked from the group of Bennet ladies to Darcy. "Why? Do you perceive that she has little else to her credit? For I have found her to be most agreeable and kind. Indeed, a more gracious woman I have not met! I would hate to think of her as the others from whom you have saved me." A shadow of pain settled on his features. "Surely, you do not think she is only after my money, do you?"

"No!" The force of Darcy's response shocked not only Bingley but Darcy as well. Calming, he continued, "I could not do such a disservice to Miss Bennet as to think of her in such a fashion. Her manners are too open, too accepting, and too honest for me to believe her capable of fortune-hunting. However," and this was the most important point of this discussion, so Darcy drew the word out to add emphasis, "it matters not what I think of her, Bingley. I wish to know your intentions. That is what I wanted to ask you yesterday. You seem smitten with her

– perhaps more than you have been with any other lady." He gave his friend what he hoped was a reassuring look, one that would hopefully stave off some of the displeasure that was certain to follow his next comments. "Are you pursuing her for honourable reasons, or are you merely toying with her affections?"

"How could you ask such a thing?" Bingley sputtered. "I would never toy with the affections of a lady such as Miss Bennet. She is not a lady of the ton who understands and seeks out a simple flirtation. I do know that paying particular attention to a lady in the country increases expectations far more quickly than it does in town. I am not without sense."

"I never said you were without sense. But there are times when your feet lead and your mind follows, and I would not wish for Miss Bennet to be injured." Darcy studied the reins in his hands. "I know too well the devastation of a lady's spirit that can result from a man's insincere attentions." He also knew how fragile Miss Bennet's heart might be. For Elizabeth's sake, he could not be a party to putting her heart in danger.

"I could never be like Wickham, Darcy. I would never injure any lady in such a fashion. My intentions are honourable."

"I did not think you would, but I needed to be reassured." So that he, in turn, and in good faith, could reassure Elizabeth. He was relieved to know he would have good news to tell her on that front when next they had an opportunity to speak privately.

"Your concern does you credit, my friend, though I am quite put out that you would think so little of my character." He eyed Darcy with mock indignation.

Darcy grinned. "Swords at dawn?"

Bingley laughed. "I will repeat; I am not without sense. That is not a challenge that I ever intend to accept. Nor shall I accept pistols or fists. I value my life, limbs, and countenance too much."

They had nearly reached Miss Bennet when Bingley cast a glance at Darcy and said in a whisper, "I believe she is my Mrs. Bingley. Do you think I am making a good choice?"

"If you love her and she loves you, then yes, she is the perfect choice. Do you love her?"

"I do."

It was only two words and they were short words at that, but the tone of assurance with which they were said and the look of calm in his friend's features let Darcy know Elizabeth had no reason to fear her sister's heart was in danger.

"Ladies," Bingley greeted as he dismounted near Miss Bennet and Darcy followed suit, "it is good to see you. We were on our way to call at Longbourn."

They were? Bingley had not shared that fact with Darcy. He looked at Bingley. His friend's attention was fully on Miss Bennet, who wore a lovely blush and a sweet smile. Bingley's future looked very promising. Darcy's eyes moved from Miss Bennet to find Miss Elizabeth.

"I have to agree. It is good to see you," he smiled at Elizabeth as he bowed his greeting.

Upon rising, he noted the men who were in the group. An officer from the militia, which had recently arrived in Meryton, stood near the youngest Bennet sisters, while two other gentlemen stood on either side of Miss Elizabeth. The first was dressed in the dark garb of a parson and the second – Darcy clenched his jaw to keep from uttering the curse that entered his mind at the sight of the scoundrel. He could feel the flush that spread rapidly up his neck and across his face.

The rogue tipped his hat slightly in Darcy's direction.

"Mr. Wickham, what brings you to Meryton?" He attempted to keep his voice within the realm of calm civility, even if it was just on the cold edge of it. His hands clenched and unclenched at his side. How he would like to snatch Wickham by his coat and remove him forcefully from the presence of Elizabeth and her sisters.

"Mr. Wickham has just joined the militia. Captain Denny was just introducing us to him."

Darcy turned his eyes to Elizabeth. She looked unsettled. Had the man done or said something to make her uneasy?

"Would you allow me to introduce our cousin to you and Mr. Bingley?" she asked.

"Of course," he replied.

"Mr. Darcy, Mr. Bingley, this is our cousin, Mr. Collins. He has only just arrived at Longbourn for a visit."

Her smile looked tight. Perhaps it was the cousin who was causing her unease.

"Mr. Collins," she continued, "this is Mr. Darcy of –"

"Pemberley in Derbyshire," Mr. Collins interrupted, giving a low, nearly grovelling, bow. "Forgive my presumption, sir, but I have the living at Hunsford, and I have often heard you spoken of with nothing but the highest praise. If I have the right of it, my esteemed patroness, Lady Catherine de Bourgh," he spoke the name with a peculiar inflection of grandeur that grated, "is your aunt, is she not?"

"Yes, she is." This fellow could most certainly be the source of Elizabeth's disquiet.

"Lady Catherine has often spoken of your mother in such lovingly affectionate terms." Mr. Collins grasped a lapel of his coat in each hand and puffed out his chest just a bit. He was certainly proud of his position, which was further off-putting to Darcy.

"She has described at length," the man continued, "just how pleased she will be to have her daughter, Miss Anne de Bourgh," there was that peculiar inflection and the drawing out of the name again, "installed as mistress of Pemberley."

"Mistress of Pemberley?" Bingley's eyes were wide in astonishment. It was a feeling Darcy shared with him.

"Yes, Mr. er..." Mr. Collins looked to Elizabeth for the name.

"Bingley," Darcy ground out. "Mr. Bingley." He held Elizabeth's gaze. She looked even more uneasy now than she had before. Collins must be the source. Something needed to be done about that man.

"Yes, Mr. Bingley," Mr. Collins said. "Miss De Bourgh and Mr. Darcy have been promised to each other for years."

"Impossible!" Bingley cried.

"I assure you it is not, Mr. Bingley." Mr. Collins' tone was utterly condescending.

Darcy closed his eyes and shook his head. The man was an idiot and his patroness, Darcy's aunt, was conniving. "I am not now, nor have I ever been, promised to my cousin or any other lady."

Mr. Collins appeared affronted. "But your aunt has assured me..."

"My aunt is mistaken," Darcy said. It was more that she was hopeful that by telling one and all that her daughter was betrothed to him, he would feel obligated to go along with the scheme. However, his aunt had underestimated Darcy's resolve to choose his own bride.

"I cannot see how she can be mistaken about something of such great importance," Mr. Collins said. "She has spoken at length about how it eases her mind to know how well you will care for Miss de Bourgh as your wife, for she approves highly of the way you have cared for your sister, though she admits there are areas where you could be more strict..." He placed a finger on his lips to prevent himself from speaking further.

Lady Catherine had spoken about Georgiana to this bumbling fool? Darcy would speak to her. A letter would be sent directly. How dare she criticize his care for his sister! Anger bubbled within him.

"How is your sister?" Wickham asked, turning Darcy's bubbling anger to fury.

He glared at Wickham with an intensity that he wished would turn him into ash. He drew a deliberately deep breath. "She is well," he replied.

"I had heard she suffered a recent disappointment and quite hoped to hear she was recovered."

"Ah, yes." Bingley left Jane's side and came to Darcy's. "Miss Darcy has recently changed companions. It can be difficult for some to adjust to change, but I believe she has adapted brilliantly. She was looking quite well when I last saw her." He placed his hand on Darcy's shoulder. "We should be on our way."

"Quite right," Darcy agreed.

"Our mother would be beyond pleased if you would join us for a cup of tea at Longbourn," Miss Bennet said.

"A cup of tea sounds delightful. Would you not agree, Darcy? Perhaps there may even be some of those delightful shortbreads. I declare that I have never had better this side of Scarborough."

Bless his friend for being so stalwartly loyal and caring. Darcy turned his back on Wickham and extended his free arm to Elizabeth. "Bingley knows I have a fondness for a well-made shortbread."

"But I wished for some ribbons for my bonnet." Miss Lydia pouted. "Denny was going to help me choose them."

"We have been gone longer than was intended already, Lydia. Your bonnet will have to wait until another day." Jane's voice and expression were firm.

It was good to see that she was not all sweetness and light but had some steeliness to her as well. She would do very well for Bingley.

Miss Lydia huffed and stamped her foot. "Come on, Kitty." She grabbed her sister's arm and strode ahead of the group. "Jane never wishes for us to have any fun!" She cast a displeased look over her shoulder.

Jane, who appeared to be entirely unruffled by her sister's display of poor behaviour, said a brief farewell to Captain Denny and Wickham for them all, and then she took Bingley's arm and followed her younger sisters. Mr. Collins scurried behind them, leaving Darcy and Elizabeth to bring up the rear of the group.

Darcy walked swiftly at first, to get as far away from Wickham as quickly as he could, but then, he slowed his pace. While he wished to be removed from the blackguard who had broken his sister's heart, he did not wish to be too close to Mr. Collins, for there were things about which he and Elizabeth needed to speak.

Chapter 4

WHEN MR. COLLINS WAS a safe distance from them, Darcy spoke softly to Elizabeth. "I am unable to explain at this moment, but it would be wise for you and your sisters to avoid Mr. Wickham. He is charming, but his character is wanting."

She glanced at him. "I had surmised that might be the case."

"Had you?" That was surprising. Most did not realize just what Wickham was until it was too late. Sadly, Darcy had to include himself in that number.

"I had."

"That is impressive. You must be an excellent discerner of character, Miss Elizabeth."

She laughed softly. "It is not so very hard to discern that a new acquaintance is one to question when a less-new acquaintance looks daggers at him. I am not certain what your relationship is with Mr. Wickham, but it seems it is not a good one."

Darcy blew out a breath. So, it had been his unguarded response that had given Wickham away. "It is not. I cannot tell you the full tale at present, but I will tell you this, in the strictest of confidence. I understand the fear you have for your sister's heart because of him."

His companion gasped. "He injured your sister?"

"Most grievously."

"And he taunted you with it!"

Darcy nodded. "That was rather bold of him."

"Indeed, it was! Oh! He is despicable!" Her anger was unmistakable. "You were very gracious to him. I am certain I would not be able to contain my fury so well as you did."

"You would if your sister's reputation depended upon it."

This comment was met with another gasp of incredulity. When he glanced in her direction, she was looking at him with tears in her eyes and simply shook her head as if there were no words to express how saddened she was to hear such a thing.

"She will be well. At least, I am hopeful that she will be."

"How could she not be?" She wiped at a tear that had escaped her rapidly blinking eyes. "She has you."

"I am not that good a brother. It was a choice that my cousin, who shares guardianship of her with me, and I made which put her in harm's way."

"I will not believe that you are not a good brother."

"But it is the truth."

"I do not see how it can be. You sat with me yesterday and listened to my story about my sister. You let me question you about your honour and the capriciousness of your friend. Then, you offered to help me protect Jane. Those are not the actions of a gentleman who has a hard heart or an unfeeling nature. I spent all of yesterday and as much of today as I could find, amid the babblings of Mr. Collins, thinking about you and your kindness to me."

She had been thinking about him? He glanced at her.

"I fear I may have judged you harshly and wrongly, based on one comment. I should have considered all of our interactions before making a judgement."

What had he said to make her dislike him? "Do I wish to know which comment?"

She blinked as if his question was one that did not need to be asked. "You do not know?"

He shook his head.

"But you looked right at me when you said it."

Oh! That comment. He swallowed. "At the assembly?"

"Yes."

"That was horrendously rude of me."

"I will not disagree."

"Nor should you. I cannot offer any acceptable explanation for my behaviour. I can only offer my apology and assure you that it was a lie. I had no desire to dance with anyone and no wish to be pleased by anyone."

"I am to put it to a foul temper, then, am I?"

"That is precisely the source." He shook his head at his own reprehensible behaviour. "I was raised to think well of myself but not to the harm of another. I am thoroughly ashamed."

Her hand grasped his arm more firmly as she stumbled over a rock in the roadway.

"Are you well?" he asked.

"Quite. It is no more than I deserve for looking at you rather than where I was going."

His lips curled into a pleased smile.

"You still startle me, sir. You are not at all what I first believed."

"Am I forgiven?"

"Am I?" she asked in answer.

"There is nothing for me to forgive. I was abominable."

"I was too hasty in my judgement. The question remains."

She was a stubborn lady, was she not? "You are forgiven."

"As are you."

"I am happy to hear it."

They walked along in companionable silence for a distance before she broke the silence with a question, bringing Darcy back from his thoughts about how much more than tolerable she was and refocusing his mind on his purpose.

"How blows the wind from the north?"

He chuckled to hear her using their code. "The wind is favourable. And how is the southern sea?"

"Peaceful and agreeable. Is it safe for me to lower my guard? Is the treasure out of danger?"

"Based on the conversation I had with the North Wind this morning, I believe all is well. You may stand down, secure in the knowledge that the treasure of the South Sea is safe."

Delight suffused her face. "You have made me an incredibly happy sister, Mr. Darcy. However, should the wind begin to blow foul, you are honour-bound to inform me."

"Without question, Miss Elizabeth." He could happily spend his whole life conversing with her and seeing to it that she was safe and well. Perhaps soon, he would be able to present himself to her as someone to consider for her husband.

"That is one potentially devastating situation averted. I pray I can avoid the next as easily, though I fear I will not be able to."

He glanced at her. If only they were not walking with a group. Then, he would be able to stop and watch her face as they conversed much like he had yesterday.

"Are you saying the southern seas are not free of all ill?"

"Yes, that is what I am saying."

"What trouble brews?"

"A foreign vessel has dropped anchor within the harbour, and I fear its intentions will not leave the port undamaged."

Darcy's brow furrowed as he attempted to reason out her meaning.

She leaned closer to him and whispered, "My cousin."

He looked first to Mr. Collins and then to Elizabeth with a question in his eyes. She was speaking of Mr. Collins?

She nodded.

Other than being pompous and obtuse, what other problem might the man pose?

"His expedition was commissioned by his great patroness with the goal of repairing a breach within the Admiral's family. It is rumoured that the foreign ship's captain has determined to marry…" She gave a sigh of exasperation. "How did you and your cousin speak in code? I find it to be quite tiring."

He chuckled. "We never told each other extended stories using code, just quick messages, though we often used code names for places and people." He glanced ahead to see who was nearby. "I think your cousin will not hear if you wish to speak more plainly."

"He is determined to marry one of his cousins and since my mother has made him aware of Mr. Bingley's attentions to Jane, I fear he has settled upon me as his choice."

"You? And him?" So great was Darcy's shock that he stopped walking. "He is so... so... well, absurd, and you are so intelligent and sensible. Could there be a more unequal match?"

A small laugh escaped her at his unguarded response.

"I believe you have the right of it, sir. I could never willingly accept such an offer, so I fear there may be a battle brewing in the southern seas."

"Would your father force such an arrangement?" Surely not. Right? Darcy's heart pinched and his chest tightened at the thought.

"I do not believe he would, but my mother will do her best to persuade him of the advantage of the match." She placed her hand on his proffered arm, and they began walking again.

"Forgive me if I offend, but what could be the advantage of a match between you and him?"

"You do not offend. It is quite simple. The foreign vessel's captain is heir to the southern seas. Should one of the admiral's daughters marry the captain, she and her mother would be assured of remaining in their home after the admiral passes."

"Ah, I see."

Darcy spoke not a word more for several moments as he pondered the situation. He could not do a thing about the entail of an estate, but he did have enough money to see Mrs. Bennet happily settled elsewhere, if need be, when her husband died. He could not imagine Elizabeth or any of her sisters married to a gentleman who held Lady

Catherine in such high esteem that he questioned Darcy's honour in proclaiming himself not betrothed to Anne. The foolish of the youngest Bennet ladies and their mother would only grow more foolish under Mr. Collins's care. There really was only one solution.

"What if you, like your sister, had an eligible suitor?" His heart beat wildly in his chest. He had hoped to have gained some assurance of acceptance before presenting his offer, but he simply could not allow Elizabeth to be put upon by the likes of Mr. Collins if he could prevent it.

He watched her brow furrow and her lips purse. "I am afraid I do not have a ready supply of suitors from which to draw."

"You only need one."

She looked at him in bewilderment. "I assure you, sir, that if I had even one possible suitor, I would have already made his presence known to my cousin."

"What about an unknown suitor? Is there not one gentleman in all of Hertfordshire who fulfills such a role?" Him, for instance.

Frustration crept into her voice. "Must I truly admit to being so undesirable?"

"Undesirable? Good heavens! I would never ask you to prevaricate in such a fashion. I fear you mistake my meaning. I was simply inquiring if there were any gentlemen to whom you might find marriage to be agreeable."

She sighed. "There are none who come to mind."

Silently, he drew in a breath. This was it. "What if it were a gentleman who was not from Hertfordshire, but who was merely a guest in the area?" He drew another quiet breath and held it while he waited for her to grasp his meaning.

"The only guests in the area – aside from the militia, of course – are my cousin, whom we have already agreed is not suitable, and..." Her eyes grew wide, and her hand came to rest on her heart. "No, that would never do," she muttered.

Darcy flinched and looked away from her to hide the pain her words brought him.

"It is not that you are unsuitable, sir," she said quickly.

Apparently, he had not hidden his disappointment very well.

"It is just that I am unsuitable. I cannot be the sort of lady someone of your status would desire to marry. I have little, by way of fortune or connections, to recommend me to so high a position as your wife. And then there is my mother. I have had my whole life to learn to love her as she is. I could not..." She shrugged rather than completing her thought. "I thank you for your kind generosity. I wish..."

She stopped once again, but this time she shook her head. "To offer to court a lady just to spare her the attentions of another? Truly, you are too noble by half."

She still did not understand him. "I do not offer to be noble, Elizabeth."

Her eyes grew wide at his use of her Christian name. He stopped walking and turned to her. They were close to Longbourn, and he did not wish for this conversation to be interrupted.

"I offer because it is what I desire."

She sucked in a sharp breath.

"I will not pretend that certain members of your family will not try my patience, nor will I say that your lack of standing and fortune will never cause an issue with my family. However, they shall not dissuade me."

She blinked twice and shook her head again. "You desire to court me?"

"I do." He took her hands in his. Shocked pleasure was in her expression, and he dared to hope he would not be refused.

"You do not fear the disapproval of your family or society?"

"I will ask you again what I asked you yesterday when we were speaking about my friend and your sister. If we were to love each other – most ardently," for he was sure he was well on his way to such a state, "would that not be enough to weather whatever trials family, fortune, and society might pose?"

"Love?" She said the word in a wondering sort of fashion as if she could not believe that he had even considered himself in love with her or that she could fathom that he would love her. No matter what the source of her wonder was, the fact remained that he was certain he loved her.

"Yes, love. Do you think you might someday be able to return my affection?"

He had not thought her eyes could grow wider, but they did.

"If," he continued, "you think you may, and if you desire to have me as a suitor, I will speak to your father directly, so that I do not have to fear your cousin's attention to you."

She chuckled at that and then grew serious. "What about your aunt and cousin?" she asked. "If they think you are betrothed, will that not pose an issue?"

"Most likely, yes. However, I do not need their approval, Elizabeth, or anyone else's. I only need yours."

She held his gaze without saying a word for what seemed like an eternity. Then, a smile slowly curled her lips and danced into her eyes. "You require more than my approval, Mr. Darcy."

He shook his head and was about to refute her comment when she arched an eyebrow in challenge, and he held his tongue.

"You need my father's."

He could not contain the joy that he felt at her words. It bubbled out of his heart and across his face in what he was sure was a ridiculous grin. "Does that mean I have your approval to speak to him?"

She nodded. "And quite likely my heart." Her cheeks grew rosy at the admission.

He lifted her hand to his lips. "I promise you, Elizabeth, that I will protect your heart with all that is in me."

His words would, of course, be put to the test. While most who heard the happy news about Darcy and Elizabeth's courtship and eventual betrothal and marriage were delighted with the match, there were a few who were not. However, no matter how Lady Catherine blustered or what taunting whispers came from Caroline or any of the other disappointed ladies of the ton, nothing and no one was ever able to break the bond that had been forged between Darcy and Elizabeth during those two days in November when they had embarked on a plan to secure the happiness of a beloved sister and friend and, in the process, had discovered their own.

If you enjoyed this book, be sure to let others know
by leaving a review.

Want to know when other Leenie books will be available?
You can always know what's new with my books by
joining one of my reader communities

leeniebrown.com/subscribe

More Books by Leenie

You can find all of Leenie's books at this link

bit.ly/LeenieBBooks
where you can explore the collections below

Dash of Darcy and Companions Collection

Marrying Elizabeth Series

Sweet Possibilities and Sweet Extras

Willow Hall Romances

The Choices Series

Darcy Family Holidays

Darcy and... An Austen-Inspired Collection

Teatime Tales (Sweet Austen-inspired Novelettes)

Other Pens

Touches of Austen

Nature's Fury and Delights (Sweet Regency Novelettes)

About Leenie

Leenie Brown has always been a girl with an active imagination, which, while growing up, was both an asset, providing many hours of fun as she played out stories, and a liability, when her older sister and aunt would tell her frightening tales. At one time, they had her convinced Dracula lived in the trunk at the end of the bed she slept in when visiting her grandparents!

Although it has been years since she cowered in her bed in her grandparents' basement, she still has an imagination which occasionally runs away with her, and she feeds it now as she did then — by reading!

Her heroes, when growing up, were authors, and the worlds they painted with words were (and still are) her favourite playgrounds! Now, as an adult, she spends much of her time in the Regency world, playing with the characters from her favourite Jane Austen novels and those of her own creation.

When she is not traipsing down a trail in an attempt to keep up with her imagination, Leenie resides in the beautiful province of Nova Scotia with her two sons and her very own Mr. Brown (a wonderful mix of all the best of Darcy, Bingley, and Edmund with a healthy dose of the teasing Mr. Tilney and just a dash of the scolding Mr. Knightley).

Connect with Leenie in one of her reader communities or on social media. Find links to all of those on her website at bit.ly/connect-with-leenie

www.ingramcontent.com/pod-product-compliance
Lightning Source LLC
Chambersburg PA
CBHW072046170626
46811CB00008B/3188